Volume 1

LAUGH OUT LOUD

Jokes and Riddles from

Highlights
for Children

Illustrated by Erin Mauterer

Published by Highlights for Children, Inc.
P.O. Box 18201
Columbus, Ohio 43218-0201
Printed in China

Publisher Cataloging-in-Publication Data (U.S.)

Laugh out loud : jokes and riddles from Highlights for Children /
illustrated by Erin Mauterer.—1st ed.
   p. : ill. ; cm.
ISBN 1-59078-347-6; Vol. 1
1. Riddles, Juvenile. 2. American wit and humor, Juvenile.
I. Highlights for children. II. Title
818.60208 dc22   PN6371.5.L374 2004

First edition, 2004
The text of this book is set in 12-point New Century Schoolbook.

Visit our Web site at www.highlights.com

10 9 8 7 6 5 4 3 2 1

Contents

5 Cowabunga

11 Sports Shorts

31 Knock, Knock

39 Grab Bag

63 All Mixed Up

77 Bee Hee-Hees

83 Out of This World

95 Wacky Wear

103 Tummy Ticklers

119 Harmonic Humor

129 Giggle Bytes

135 Brain Bogglers

147 Are We There Yet?

161 Cackle Soup

169 Scared Silly

193 Funny Bones

203 Laugh Lessons

221 Witty Weather

227 This and That

251 Grins à la Mode

256 Share the Fun

What's the world's biggest
  milkshake?
A cow on a trampoline.

Heather Lyell—Indiana

Why did the cow cross the road?
To get to the udder side.

Jamie Fisher—Oregon

What's black and white and very
dangerous?
A cow on a skateboard.

Bradley Biron—Vermont

What has four legs and says,
"Oom, oom"?
A cow walking backward.

Ashley Mackes—New Hampshire

When is long hair like milk?
*When it's pasteurized (past your
eyes).*

Sherry and Janis Spidle—Missouri

Do you know how long cows should
be milked?
The same as short ones.

Ira Jay Cohen—New York

What do you call a cow that just
   had a baby?
De-calf-inated.

What subject do cow students
   like best?
Moosic.

Monica Neuhauser—Indiana

What do you call a cattle trailer
   with nothing in it?
A cattle-lack.

Terri King—Missouri

Where does a cow get its medicine?
From a farmacy.

Aaron Brenzel—Arizona

What is a cow's favorite fruit?
Cattleloupe.

Tyler Shuster—California

What happens when a cow walks
through a bramble patch?
An udder catastrophe.

Jaclyn Ash—Texas

How do you keep milk from getting
sour?
You leave it in the cow.

David Rodriguez—Arizona

What do you get when you cross a
chicken and a cow?
Roost beef.

Crystal Kuch—Massachusetts

What does a cow say at night?
"Mooooon."

Andrew Steinkraus—Washington

What do you call a queen who plays
 golf?
The queen of clubs.

Allison Krichman—New Jersey

What do you call a boomerang that
  doesn't come back?
A stick.

Kacey Kirch—Minnesota

Jim: "What's your business?"
Pat: "Bowling."
Jim: "How do you like it?"
Pat: "It's right up my alley."

Cassandra Cox—South Carolina

Where would a pitcher not want
  to wear red?
In the bullpen.

Jason Amaro—Kansas

Mark: "My favorite team is the
  Red Sox."
Kathy: "I like the White Sox."
Ashley: "Well, I like nylons. They
  get more runs."

Ashley Olson—Massachusetts

Daughter: "Mom, where are you going?"

Mom: "I'm going jogging as soon as I stretch out my legs."

Daughter: "Why? Are they too short?"

Brooke Saba—New Hampshire

What happened when the two ropes played a football game?
They tied.

Nora Ivory—Maryland

What exercises can you do in the water?
Pool-ups.

Kaitlin Barr—Ohio

Which athletes are the sloppiest
  eaters?
*Basketball players, because they
  dribble so much.*

Laura Douglas—Nebraska

Where do soccer players like to sit
   in a movie theater?
In the ball-cony.

Adam Jenkins—Virginia

What runs around a baseball field but never moves?
A fence.

Natasha Capparuccia—North Carolina

Coach: "What do you drink before a marathon?"
Athlete: "Lots of running water."

Hanh Lam—Colorado

Does it take longer to run from first to second base or from second to third base?
Second to third base because there is a short stop between them.

Tommy Roseman—Ohio

Greg: "Why don't you play golf with Toni anymore?"

Bob: "Would you play with someone who moves the ball when you're not looking and writes down the wrong scores?"

Greg: "Certainly not."

Bob: "Neither would Toni."

James Fields—Texas

How does glue run?
At a slow paste.

Rachel Nuell—Virginia

How do ears stay fit?
With earobics.

Jaya Saxena—New York

What kind of dog plays football?
A golden receiver.

John O'Neill—Massachusetts

Scuba store clerk: "What can I get for you?"

Customer: "Tanks."

Scuba store clerk: "Oh, that's very polite, but I didn't get you anything yet."

Billy Stokes—New York

What can you serve but not eat?
A tennis ball.

Pedro Bastos—Minnesota

Sara: "Are you coming to the
baseball game?"
Sam: "No, I know what the score
will be before it starts."
Sara: "What will it be?"
Sam: "Zero to zero."

Sathya Sridharan—Missouri

Pam: "Why are you doing the
backstroke?"
Sam: "I just had lunch, and I
don't want to swim on a full
stomach."

Jay Choi—Virginia

Don: "Ann, why are you crying?"
Ann: "My bowling ball is broken."
Don: "How do you know?"
Ann: "It has holes in it."

Ronnie Dube—Pennsylvania

Peter: "Hey Joe, I went riding this morning."
Joe: "Horseback?"
Peter: "Yes, it got back two hours before I did."

Joey Feyoo—New York

What does a football player eat soup from?
A Super Bowl

Bridget Ryals—Mississippi

Why did the chicken wear a
  tuxedo?
He was going to a fowl ball.

Andrew Pittman—Virginia

Why did the basketball coach flood
   the gym?
*He wanted his team to sink some
   baskets.*

A. J. Coggins and
Kayleen Chugg—Arizona

Little brother: "Thanks for the baseball cards, but I can't read yet."

Big brother: "That's OK. You can still look at the pitchers."

David Grace—Colorado

Why do soccer players do so well in school?

They always use their heads.

Nic Lundberg—Washington

Billy: "May I go swimming?"

Mom: "No, you should wait a half-hour because you just ate."

Billy: "But I had fish."

Kristan and Megen Files
—Massachusetts

Why is a basketball game equal to
   a dollar?
Both are made up of four quarters.

Andrew Close—Washington

Why did the football coach send in
   his second string?
To tie up the game.

Tara Stone—Missouri

Joanne: "Hey, Matt, may I use
   your sled?"
Matt: "Sure. We'll split it half-and-
   half."
Joanne: "Thanks!"
Matt: "You use it uphill, and I'll
   use it downhill."

Randell Adarme—California

What's the easiest thing to catch
    when you're ice fishing?
A cold.

Brandon Champion—Mississippi

Why did the basketball player
  bring a suitcase to the game?
In case she traveled.

Gautam Sane—Texas

What is the world's longest
   punctuation mark?
The hundred-yard dash.

Tracie Taft—Vermont

What baseball team does a jokester
   like best?
The New York Prankees.

Levi Squier—Connecticut

Sam: "Did you hear about the guy
   who bought a new boomerang?"
Joe: "No, what about him?"
Sam: "He had a hard time throwing
   the old one away."

Waylon Lampson—Wisconsin

Fred: "I know a couple who talk in their sleep. He plays golf, and she goes to auction sales."

Albert: "Really?"

Fred: "Yes. Just the other night he yelled, 'Fore!' then she yelled, 'Four fifty!'"

Brynn Martin—Ohio

The ticket seller at a high-school basketball game let in the chicken, the turkey, the pheasant, and the goose, but he turned away the duck. Why?

Five fowls and you're out.

Andrew Dean—Virginia

Knock, Knock

Knock, knock.
Who's there?
Little old lady.
Little old lady who?
I didn't know you could yodel.

Jami Green—Oklahoma

Knock, knock.
Who's there?
Eddie.
Eddie who?
Eddie-body got a tissue? I have a
    terrible cold!

Jennifer Hennes—Wisconsin

Knock, knock.
Who's there?
Icon.
Icon who?
Icon make you open the door.

Billy Zammarrelli—New Jersey

Knock, knock.
Who's there?
Soup.
Soup who?
Souper man!

Kevin Amaral—Massachusetts

Knock, knock.
Who's there?
Drew.
Drew who?
Drew you a picture. Want to see it?

Umair Ali—Ontario

Knock, knock.
Who's there?
Army.
Army who?
Army and you still pals?

Greg Chrisis—Massachusetts

Knock, knock.
Who's there?
Philippa.
Philippa who?
Philippa plate and dig in.

Jackie Guerrero—Hawaii

Knock, knock.
Who's there?
A little boy who can't reach
the doorbell.

Ja'Quoi Griffin—Michigan

Knock, knock.
Who's there?
Cargo.
Cargo who?
Cargo beep beep.

Justin Manley—Virginia

Sadie: "Would you know me if you didn't see me for a day?"
Sally: "Sure!"
Sadie: "Knock, knock."
Sally: "Who's there?"
Sadie: "See, you've forgotten me already."

Elaine Borkholder—Indiana

Knock, knock.
Who's there?
Arnie.
Arnie who?
Arniements are fun to put on
    the tree.

Kyle Saunders—Newfoundland

Knock, knock.
Who's there?
Sasha.
Sasha who?
Sasha fuss, just because I knock at
    your door!

Justin Patterson—Connecticut

Why did the man wear a bathing
  suit to work?
Because he was in a car pool.

Margarita Tristani—Puerto Rico

There was a building that was forty-eight stories tall. Some people say that it was forty-nine stories tall, but that's another story.

Ashley Beach—Georgia

How do you know that heat is
  faster than cold?
You can catch a cold.

What is the world's silliest
  invention?
The solar-powered flashlight.

Matthew Hofer—Minnesota

Kim: "Did you hear about the
  man who stayed up all night
  wondering where the Sun goes
  after it sets?"
Tim: "No, what happened?"
Kim: "It finally dawned on him."

Michelle White—South Carolina

How can you go without sleep for
  seven days?
Sleep at night.

Jessica Raymond—Virginia

What do you buy for someone who
  has everything?
A burglar alarm.

John Pitt—New Jersey

Tina: "What would happen if you
  had no ears?"
Joel: "I wouldn't be able to see."
Tina: "You mean you wouldn't be
  able to hear."
Joel: "No, I wouldn't be able to see.
  My hat would fall over my eyes."

Ali Bin Hashim—Iowa

Mary: "You look pretty dirty."
Anne: "Yes, and I look even prettier clean."

Catherine Young—British Columbia

Where does a lumberjack go to buy things?

The chopping center.

David Peters—Georgia

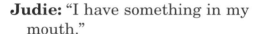

Judie: "I have something in my mouth."

Sarah: "What is it? A bug?"

Judie: "No, it's my tongue!"

Emily Aeschliman—Indiana

Mr. Wright: "Can I put this wallpaper on myself?"

Clerk: "Yes, but it looks better on the wall."

Michael Dvorak—Minnesota

Clint: "I think I'm turning into a bridge!"

Clara: "What has come over you?"

Clint: "So far, two trucks and a bus."

Mike Montgomery—Washington

What is stucco?
What you get when you sit in gummo.

Tierney Brown—Oklahoma

Why did Humpty Dumpty have a great fall?
To make up for a bad summer.

Ernest Yang—Washington

Dan: "Did you go to the grocery store for your mother?"
Fran: "No, I went for groceries."

Linda Jo Lonaberger—Pennsylvania

What kind of deal does a dog hate?
A flea bargain.

Devon Rex—Texas

What do you call a carousel without brakes?

A merry-go-round-round-round. . . .

Priyanka Shivakumar—New Jersey

Billy: "What are you doing with that watering can?"

Benny: "I want to water my flowers."

Billy: "But it's raining outside."

Benny: "That's all right. I have my raincoat on."

Leah Fisch—New York

Kim: "Have you heard about the three holes in the ground?"
Tim: "No."
Kim: "Well, well, well."

Cristina Lalonde—Massachusetts

A dog was tied to a fifteen-foot rope, but she walked thirty feet. How did she do it?
The rope wasn't tied to anything.

Kathy McGill—Illinois

Son: "Mom, are you going to be on the six o'clock news tomorrow?"
Mom: "Yes, I am."
Son: "Great! What time does it start?"

Allan Claros—Oklahoma

Brenda: "You put too many stamps on that letter."

Michele: "Oh no. Now it will go too far!"

Viviane Tamagnone—Connecticut

We were born together. We live one inch apart. We see everything, but we cannot see each other. Who are we?

Eyes.

Sanah Ali—New York

Kelly: "Don't just sit there like a bump on a log. Do something!"

Bump: "Well, I am a bump, and I'm only doing my job."

Nikki Gallion—North Carolina

Why did the
   detective carry a flashlight?
Because he wanted to shed some
   light on the case.

Marshall Roorda—Missouri

A man walked into an antique shop. He went up to the sales clerk and asked, "So, what's new?"

Meera Patel—Illinois

Lucy: "Which burns longer, a red candle or a green one?"
Sam: "Neither. They both burn shorter."

Sagebelle Wu—Taiwan

A man walks into a store and asks the clerk for a dead battery, so the clerk gets one for him. When the man asks how much it costs, the clerk answers, "No charge."

Ben Zolkower—Tennessee

Julie: "I used to be a stand-up comedian before I switched jobs."
Kim: "Why did you switch jobs?"
Julie: "My feet got tired."

Julie Smith—Vermont

How do you know when a train has
  passed by?
It leaves its tracks behind.

Duke Fogle—Michigan

How does a lump of coal start a
  story?
"Once upon a mine. . . ."

Robyn-Lanae Thames—North Carolina

Why is a dog so hot in the summer?
Because it wears a coat and pants.

Marisa Temple—Missouri

Why did the lady put lipstick on
  her head?
She wanted to make up her mind.

Beth Malone—Colorado

Why shouldn't you iron a four-leaf clover?
You don't want to press your luck.

Jamye Durrance—Florida

What do you call a meeting of irons?

A press conference.

Andrew Wallin—Florida

What do you call a book that only has pages with even numbers? *Odd*.

Lindsay Egan—New York

Thomas: "I'm very intelligent."
Gracie: "Really? What makes you so smart?"
Thomas: "Three things. The first thing is my great memory, and the other two things . . . I just forgot!"

Noah Stephens—Oregon

Kim: "What did the trapeze artist do on his vacation?"
Jinny: "He really let go."

Jethro Mariano—California

Cindy: "I can see into the future."
Lisa: "When did this start?"
Cindy: "Next Monday."

Jeremy Ruppel—Michigan

Why couldn't the bike stand
  by itself?
Because it was two tired.

Vince Montpetit—Minnesota

Tyler: "I'm in trouble."
Kristopher: "Why?"
Tyler: "I've lost my glasses, and
  I can't look for them until I've
  found them."

Katelyn Grieder—Pennsylvania

What did King Arthur say to his court?

"I want all of you to enroll in knight school."

Jennifer Thompson—Alberta

Cody: "Who got first prize in the beauty contest?"
Morgan: "The winner."

Sean Clancy—New York

What disasters happen every
twenty-four hours?
Day breaks and night falls.

Elise Haase—Oregon

Carol: "I made these socks for my
brother at college."
Ellen: "They're lovely, but why did
you knit three socks?"
Carol: "In his last letter he said
he'd grown another foot."

Roland Flora—Pennsylvania

Which business person drives
customers away?
A taxi driver.

Ramzey El Gadi—California

What happens when you throw a
green rock into the Red Sea?
It gets wet.

How did the judge find out about
the rotten milk?
There was an odor in the quart.

Jordan Ames—Texas

What did Billy say after he learned
how to count money?
"It all makes cents now."

Masha Kargopoltseva—Washington

What do you get when you cross
an alligator with a pickle?
A crocodill.

Leanna Chen—British Columbia

What do you get when you cross
an octopus with an armadillo?
An eight-arm-adillo.

David Johnston—Alberta

What do you get when you cross
   a duck with a rooster?
An animal that wakes you up at the
   quack of dawn.

Brenna Doyle—Indiana

What do you get when you cross
   an elephant and a dog?
A very nervous mailman.

Corey Smith—Oklahoma

What do you get when you cross
   a saber-toothed tiger with
   a flower?
I don't know, but I wouldn't smell it.

Ryan Petrello—Maryland

What do you get when you cross
   a centipede with a parrot?
A walkie-talkie.

Martin Bronson—New York

What do you get if you cross an
   elephant with a skunk?
*I don't know, but you can smell it
coming from miles away.*

Celeste Authement—Louisiana

What do you get when you cross
   a basketball with a groundhog?
*Six more weeks of basketball
season.*

Amanda Stanley—California

What do you get when you cross
  an elephant with a fish?
Swimming trunks.

Ashley Smith—Washington

What do you get when you cross
a watermelon with a bus?
*A watermelon that can seat
forty-five people.*

Ben Mackowski—Arizona

What do you get when you cross
a rabbit with a spider web?
A hare net.

Kristin Lavelle—Pennsylvania

What do you get when you combine
electricity with a car?
A Voltswagen.

Luke Mayes—Montana

What do you get when you cross
a praying mantis and a termite?
*A bug that says grace before eating
your house.*

Lydia Adi—California

What do you get when you cross
    a quarter and a car?
A coinvertible.

What do you get when you cross
    a hummingbird with a
    doorbell?
A humdinger.

Lauren Anderson—North Carolina

What do you get when you cross
    a parrot and a yak?
A yakety-yak.

Che-Che Crizaldo—Philippines

What do you get if you cross a
   dinosaur and a football player?
A quarterback no one can tackle.

Sean Borruso—New York

What do you get
    when you cross
    a dachshund with
    a giraffe?
A right angle.

Adam Beauchamp—Georgia

What do you get when you cross
poison ivy and a four-leaf
clover?
A rash of good luck.

Kristina Lersbuasin—Oregon

What do you get when you cross
a kangaroo and a sheep?
A sweater with big pockets.

Joseph McCudden—Illinois

What do you get when you cross
a telephone with a pair of
pants?
Bell-bottoms.

Cara Di Quinzio—Rhode Island

What do you get when you cross
 two banana peels?
A pair of slippers.

Kevin Hood—Georgia

What do you get when you cross
 a kangaroo with a snake?
A jump rope.

Michaele Frank—South Carolina

What do you get when you cross
 binoculars with a shell?
A see-shell.

Joe Andreoni—Wisconsin

What do get when you cross a goat
 with a clown?
A silly goat.

Kelsea Pennington—Alabama

What do you get when you cross
   a lion and a porcupine?
*Something you don't want to sit
   next to on the bus.*

Julie Fromm—Washington

What do you get when you cross
   a rainstorm and a convertible?
A carpool.

Rachel Snare—Minnesota

What do you get when you cross
   a monkey with a pie?
A meringue-atang.

Travis Whelpley—New Mexico

What do you get when you cross
   a cow and an octopus?
*A farm animal that can milk
   itself.*

John Haseman—Illinois

Why are bees happy when they
  get married?
Because they can go on a honeymoon.

Joshua Allaire—Maine

What did the bee say to the flower?
"What time do you open?"

Beau Niec—Wisconsin

What's better than a dog that can count?
A spelling bee.

Leslie Armistead—Tennessee

How do bees go to school?
By the buzz!

Lin Fu—New York

What do you call a bee with a low buzz?
A mumble bee.

Julia Ballis—Massachusetts

What do bees do when they are proud of each other?
They give each other hive-fivezzzz.

Thomas Young—Florida

What do bees chew?
Bumble gum.

Lara Carrier—Pennsylvania

What did the worker bee say to the
   queen bee?
"You are bee-utiful."

Ashley Gustin—Kansas

What do you call a confused
   bumblebee?
Buzzled.

Andrew Lee—New York

What does a bee wear when it
   dresses up?
A yellow jacket.

Michelle O'Shepa—Massachusetts

Why did the bee go south for the
  winter?
To visit an ant in Florida.

Alex Mitrani—New York

Where do bees go when they get
 hurt?
To the waspital.

Joey Gambardella—New Jersey

What's the best thing for hives?
Bees.

Stacy Wall—Illinois

What does a bee use to style its
 hair?
A honeycomb.

Maggie Yu—New York

Out of This World

Pat: "Did you hear about the restaurant on the moon?"
Dave: "No. What about it?"
Pat: "It has good food but no atmosphere."

Kieran Tintle—New Jersey

Marge: "Can you telephone from the space shuttle?"

Alice: "Of course I can tell a telephone from the space shuttle. The phone's the one with the long cord."

Jessica St. Clair—Florida

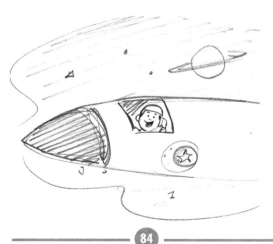

Where did the alien put her
  teacup?
On a flying saucer.

Taylor Harrison—California

How does the man in the moon get
  his hair cut?
Eclipse it.

Elyse Goike—Michigan

What do space aliens eat for
  breakfast?
Flying sausages.

Daniel Metzel—Virginia

Why does the moon go to the bank?
To change quarters.

Danielle Evans—New Jersey

What are the clumsiest things in
   the galaxy?
Falling stars.

Sarah Wood—Ontario

How many balls of string would it
   take to reach the moon?
*Just one, but it would have to be
   a big one.*

Catherine Rosenberg—Maryland

First astronaut: "Let's go to the
   moon."
Second astronaut: "We can't."
First astronaut: "Why not?"
Second astronaut: "It's a full
   moon."

Danny Kwon—California

What does Saturn like to read?
Comet books.

Timmy White—Washington

What do astronauts eat when they
are in space?
Star fruit.

Jose Perez—Florida

What do you say to a two-headed
   space alien?
"Hello, hello!"

Why should you never insult a
   Martian?
It might get its feelers hurt.

  Meleah Madsen—Washington

What do moon men call french
   fries?
Crater taters.

  Maren Woodward—Alaska

What flowers grow in outer space?
Sunflowers.

  Khalid Islam—Pennsylvania

Can Saturn take a bath?
Yes, but it will leave a ring around the tub.

Sydney Spencer—California

After landing on Earth, a space alien saw a bird. The alien asked, "How much does it cost to stay in a hotel?"

"Cheep, cheep," said the bird.

"Good," said the alien, "because it cost me a fortune to get here!"

Zachary Balsky—Michigan

How do you have a good outer space party?
Plan-it.

Angie Casertano—Florida

How did Mary's little lamb get to
   Mars?
By rocket sheep.

Samantha Probasco—Iowa

A woman pulled up to a gas station and started putting gas in her car. Pretty soon, a spaceship landed and an alien got out. The woman noticed the letters UFO on the side of the ship, so she asked the alien, "Does UFO stand for unidentified flying object?"

"No," said the alien, "it stands for unleaded fuel only."

Kimberly Froelich—Illinois

What is an alien's favorite dish?
A flying saucer.

Richard Yao—New York

What was the first animal in
  space?
*The cow that jumped over the
  moon.*

Joe Greenwood—Alabama

What happens when an astronaut
  lets go of his ice cream?
He gets an ice-cream float.

Alex Beard—Indiana

Why didn't the rocket have a job?
Because it was fired on Monday.

Amber Deshields—South Carolina

Why did the cow use a spaceship?
To get to the Milky Way.

Annie Klassen—British Columbia

What kind of music do they play on
a space shuttle?
Rocket-roll.

James Neubauer—Indiana

What letter will set a star in
motion?
The letter T makes star start.

Lucille Chevrier—Quebec

How is food served to the man in
the moon?
In a satellite dish.

Andrew Bowers—Illinois

Customer: "I'd like to try on that dress in the window."

Storekeeper: "Fine, but we'd rather have you try it on in the dressing room."

Malky Drew—New York

What do you call a hat that you
   wear on your knee?
A kneecap.

Adam Dunigan—California

What do you call a man wearing
an alphabet suit?
A letter carrier.

Jonathan Wolf—New Jersey

What do you say to a tailor about
his clothes?
"Suit yourself."

Shaylee Lamb—Tennessee

Ginny: "What's on your foot?"
Robbie: "A shoe."
Ginny: "Gesundheit!"

Virginia Mae Moore—Pennsylvania

What's another name for a raincoat?
A drench coat.

Joe King—Utah

What has two legs but doesn't walk?

A pair of pants.

Christopher Mata—Florida

Megan: "Mom, can I go out and play?"

Mom: "With those awful holes in your socks?"

Megan: "No, with the kids next door."

Janae Swartzlander—Missouri

Where does the king keep his armies?

In his sleevies.

Katie and Tom Goeke—Kentucky

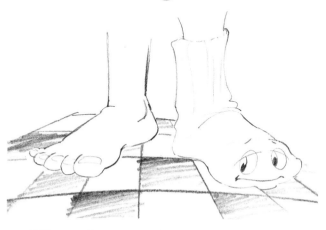

Where does a sock go when it loses
 its partner?
To the repair shop.

Regina Loflin—Mississippi

Where do cats put their dirty
clothes?
In the ham-purr.

Matt Levi Tuttle—Iowa

Salesman: "That suit fits you like a glove."

Customer: "Can you show me one that fits like a suit?"

Julia Drubinskaya—Illinois

Ernest: "I'd like to buy a pair of long johns."

Storekeeper: "How long do you want them?"

Ernest: "Oh, from about September to February."

Becky Cassidy—Vermont

What has lots of eyes, two tongues, and stinks?

A pair of old tennis shoes.

Billy Black—Kentucky

How do you make pants last?
Make the coat first.

Becky Williams—Michigan

Ted: "Do you have holes in your
   pants?"
John: "No, of course not."
Ted: "Then how do you get your
   feet in?"

Albert Shalom—New York

What has a neck but no head,
   arms but no hands, and a waist
   but no legs?
A T-shirt.

Cameron Vea—California

Sister: "Why are you dancing on the peanut butter jar?"

Brother: "Because it said 'Twist to open.'"

Brook Haughs—Indiana

What is green and dangerous?
A thundering herd of pickles.

Rachel Carroll—Massachusetts

How do you fix a broken pizza?
With tomato paste.

Brendon Myer—Pennsylvania

Girl: "Dad, are we having burgers on the grill?"
Dad: "No, I think they would be better on plates!"

Mercedes Rosado—North Dakota

Why didn't the man buy the bakery?
He couldn't raise the dough.

Chris Mulloy—New York

Where does smart butter go?
On the honor roll.

Kelli Whitman—New Jersey

How did the knife beat the fork home?

It took a shortcut.

Damon Bailey—Arkansas

Why doesn't cream cheese ever lose a card game?

It's always on a roll.

T. J. Pfister—Indiana

How did the eggs cross the road?

They scrambled.

Dana Josephs—Massachusetts

Why did the little boy throw peanut butter into the ocean?

To go with the jellyfish.

Morgan Husen—Michigan

How do you get a giant into
   a frying pan?
Use shortening.

Amber Fenoglio—Illinois

What bird is at every meal?
A *swallow*.

Rachel Lennon—Tennessee

Blair: "Have you heard the story about the stick of butter?"

Jenny: "No."

Blair: "Never mind. I don't want to spread it around."

Elizabeth Haynes—Oklahoma

A clerk living in Canada works in a butcher shop. He is 5 feet 11 inches tall. What does he weigh?

He weighs meat.

Scott Stewart—Germany

Big Sister: "Eat your spinach. It will put color in your cheeks."

Little Sister: "Who wants green cheeks, anyway!"

Gregory Lusk—Ohio

Bob: "Does your dog Ginger bite?"
Max: "No. Ginger snaps."

Raymond Chan—Alberta

What kind of garden does a baker have?
A flour garden.

Casey Zielinski and Beth Vogt—Illinois

Teacher: "Billy, what are the four seasons?"
Billy: "Salt, pepper, sugar, and spice."

Andrew Vial—Tennessee

What do you call a lazy butcher?
A meat loafer.

Carley Hansen—Washington

How do you make a hot dog stand?
Take away its chair.

Neil Matsuzaki—California

What do you get when you eat
crackers in bed?
A crumby night's sleep.

Vicky Richards—Washington

Why is bread lots of fun?
It's made of "wheeeat."

Tina: "Do you knead dough to make bread?"
Doug: "Of course you need dough to make bread."

Michelle DuBois—Wisconsin

What kind of jokes does popcorn love?
Corny ones.

Melvin Johnson—California

What is green and sings?
Elvis Parsley.

Nicholas Menis—New York

How do you make ice laugh?
You just pour water on it, and it cracks up.

Benjamin Blum—Taiwan

What did Baby Corn say to Mama Corn?
"Where is Pop Corn?"

Sean Chatterson—Saskatchewan

Why didn't the omelet laugh?
It didn't get the yolk.

Jennifer Spencer—Indiana

What is the best butter in the world?
A goat.

Ramon Soto—California

What did the hamburger name its
   daughter?
Patty.

Jacob Apodaca—Texas

Where does bread go to work?
To the toast office.

Beth Conway—Ohio

Steve: "Dad, did you hear the watermelon joke?"
Dad: "No, Son, I didn't."
Steve: "It's pitiful."

Garrett DiCarlo—Massachusetts

Where can a burger get a great night's sleep?
On a bed of lettuce.

Kristle Shepherd—Washington, D.C.

What does the invisible man like to drink?
Evaporated milk.

Kris Ashrafi—California

Why did the man eat the candle?
He wanted a light snack.

Drew Albers—Missouri

Kate: "I know what you had for dinner."
Samantha: "OK, what did I have?"
Kate: "You had tomato soup with a grilled cheese sandwich."
Samantha: "Did my mom tell you that?"
Kate: "No, your shirt did."

Claire Huber—New York

When does a soda bottle catch cold?
When it stands around with its cap off.

Katheryn Casuga—Virginia

Harmonic Humor

What kind of band do whales
   play in?
An orca-stra.

Ryan Davenport—Wisconsin

Where do rabbits go when they
 want to hear singing?
To the hop-era.

Marjorie Boivin—Michigan

Patient: "Doctor, I was playing my flute when suddenly I swallowed it!"

Doctor: "Well, look on the bright side. You could have been playing a piano."

Patrick McIntire—Germany

Why does a waxed floor remind you of music?

Because if you don't C-sharp, you'll B-flat.

Ivan Liang—New York

What does a singer need to become an opera star?

An opera-tune-ity.

Audrey Decherd—Texas

Bill: "Where's your new guitar?"
Sam: "I had to throw it away."
Bill: "Why did you do that?"
Sam: "Because there was a hole in the middle of it."

Belinda Liu—Connecticut

What kind of music do angels listen to?
Soul music.

Josef Kozij—Arkansas

Why couldn't Mozart find his teacher?
His teacher was Haydn.

Ashley Equi—Wisconsin

What do you call a bunch of tires
   that play music?
A rubber band.

Nikki Parrish—Pennsylvania

What sea animal is the most
   musical?
A fiddler crab.

Kathleen Connors—British Columbia

What kind of teacher teaches how
   to play the flute?
A private tooter.

Hillary Welsh—Nevada

Pat: "I once sang 'The Star-
   Spangled Banner' for three hours
   nonstop."
Shannon: "That's nothing. I can
   sing 'Stars and Stripes Forever.' "

Jenny Urbanczyk—Texas

When do you use a bow without an
   arrow?
When you're playing the violin.

Anne Aderman—Colorado

What sea animal can sing the best?
An octave-pus.

Briana Baker—Kansas

Band student: "Our school played
  Beethoven last night."
Gym student: "Who won?"

Jessica Wandrie—Michigan

What did the violin maker say
  when he made a mistake?
"Oh, fiddlesticks!"

Meagan Johnson—Connecticut

How did the flute know what it
  had to say?
It made notes.

Nicole Rathmann—Illinois

Violinist: "When can I use the
    practice room?"
Pianist: "I'll be out in a minuet."

David Foster—British Columbia

What music do kids like to hear on
  their birthdays?
New Age music.

Dan O'Connor—Pennsylvania

Which instrument plays only sour
  notes?
The pickle-o.

Diana Maldonado—Connecticut

A father listened to his seven-
year-old son play his violin while
the dog howled miserably nearby.
Finally he asked the boy, "Can't you
play anything that the dog doesn't
know?"

Renee Posey—Louisiana

Why can't a cat use a computer?
It keeps chasing the mouse.

David Yaffe—North Carolina

What do pigs put in their
    computers?
Sloppy disks.

Robert Wojahn—Colorado

What do computers do in Hawaii?
Surf the Net.

Alexandra Chabun—Saskatchewan

How did the gnat send the ant a
   computer message?
By flea-mail.

Daniel Ahlers—Florida

Why didn't the fly land on the
   computer?
*He thought he might get stuck on
   the World Wide Web.*

Ahuva Schwartz—New York

Where do computers go to dance?
A disk-o.

Monica Patel—Alabama

What do fish fear about computers?
Getting caught in the Internet.

Ryan Ovalle—Texas

What do you call a computer super-
  hero?
A screen saver.

Michelle Nitzahn—California

What does a baby computer call its
  father?
Data.

Lavyne Wieting—South Dakota

What is the biggest font that you
  will find on any computer?
Ele-font.

Aron Novoseletsky—Colorado

crunch...

crunch

What is a
  computer's favorite snack?
Micro chips.

Paul Mohnke—Michigan

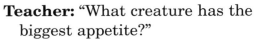

Teacher: "What creature has the biggest appetite?"
Webster: "My computer. It takes millions of bytes and never gets full."

Katie Greenwood—Maryland

Why did the robot win the dance contest?
Because he was a dancing machine.

Meagan Dixon—Ohio

What did the robot say when he ran out of electricity?
"AC come, AC go."

Joshua Fluty—South Carolina

How could a cowboy ride in on Friday, stay three days, then ride out on Friday?

Friday was the name of his horse.

Tierney Kain—Virginia

When the day after tomorrow is yesterday, today will be as far from Tuesday as today was from Tuesday when the day before yesterday was tomorrow. What day is it?

Tuesday.

Angela Drymala—Texas

What goes up and never comes
down?
Age.

Patience Andrew—Nigeria

What doesn't exist but has a name?
Nothing.

Alyssa Taylor—Washington

I grow in winter, I die in the
summer, and my roots hang in
the air. What am I?
An icicle.

Netty Friedman—New York

What room can no one enter?
A mushroom.

William Luna—Florida

What breaks but never falls? What falls but never breaks?
Dawn breaks but never falls; night falls but never breaks.

Favian Rodriguez—California

A boy just moved to a new house and made a new friend. The new friend needs to use the bathroom. There are four closed doors—a bathroom and three bedrooms. The friend picks the bathroom door without hesitating, but the boy said nothing to him. How does he know which door is the bathroom?
He used to live in that house.

Ayla Hurley—Maryland

What's harder to catch the faster
   you run?
Your breath.

Courtney Hampton—Nebraska

You're in a dark room with only one match. There is a candle, a fireplace, a stove, and a lantern. What do you light first?

The match.

Jamie Coder—Virginia

Forward I'm heavy; backward I'm
  not. What am I?
A ton.

Peter Gordon—Maryland

What can go for thousands of miles
  but never moves?
A road.

Jeremy Carlson—New York

What is put on the table and cut
  but not eaten?
A deck of cards.

Obi Otto—Palau

What's white when it's dirty?
A chalkboard.

Bailey Murphy—Alabama

What still crawls at age five?
A snake.

Melanie King—Virginia

What kind of room has no walls, a
   green floor, and a ceiling?
A mushroom.

Niko Sesno—California

What breaks when you say its
   name?
Silence.

Jennifer Robertson—Missouri

Two wrongs don't make a right, but
   what do two rights make?
Two Wrights make an airplane.

Gina Longo—New Jersey

What's the first thing a ball does
  when it stops rolling?
It looks round.

Levi Osborne—Kentucky

Two fathers and two sons order three hamburgers. Each person gets a hamburger. How?
There are only three people—a grandfather, a father, and a son.

Sebastian Hausberger—New York

What inventions have helped
  people get up in the world?
*The elevator, the escalator, and the
  alarm clock.*

Skid Laubert—Ohio

Name this vegetable: You throw
  away the outside, cook the inside,
  eat the outside, and throw away
  the inside.
Corn on the cob.

Lauren Foote—Virginia

What is it that looks like a cat, eats
  like a cat, and walks like a cat
  but is not a cat?
A kitten.

Therese Barnes—North Dakota

What has three *E*s in it but only
   one letter?
An envelope.

Michaela Levasseur—New Hampshire

What can't be used until it's
   broken?
An egg.

Vinit Jani—New York

What gets wetter the more it dries?
A towel.

Melanie Ellison—Colorado

What is easy to get into but hard to
   get out of?
Trouble.

David Mowry—Illinois

Are We There Yet?

It's so hot in Arizona that people take turns sitting in one another's shadows.

Cecelia Davis—Virginia

Why does the Statue of Liberty
stand in New York Harbor?
Because she can't sit down.

Katelyn Schuit—Illinois

Kristina: "I've got a friend in Alaska."

Melinda: "Nome?"

Kristina: "Of course I know him!"

Melinda: "No, I mean Nome in Alaska."

Kristina: "Sure, I'd know him anywhere!"

Kristina and Melinda Kuzlik—Connecticut

Which college has the best view of Los Angeles?

UCLA (You see L.A.).

Benjamin Wells—Nebraska

Where do American snakes live?

In the U.SSSSSS.A.

Batul Kassamali—California

Teacher: "Where are the Great Plains located?"
Amy: "At the great airport."

Theresa Keith—Washington

Teacher: "Children, open your geography books. Who can tell me where South America is?"
Sandy: "I can. It's on page 15."

Jason Schembri—California

If fish lived on land, where would they live?
Finland.

Brian Martin—Pennsylvania

What's the best way to see Europe
  in the morning?
Look in the mirror and you'll see
  Europe (you're up).

Linnea Bruce and
Brittany Hubbard—Missouri

A man who was going to Atlantic City saw a sign saying ATLANTIC CITY LEFT. So he turned around and went home.

Shannon Holmes—Pennsylvania

What do you call a town with 50,000 eggs?
New Yolk City.

Adam Muth—California

Which country's name is a verb?
Togo.

Rachael Menson—Ghana

Where do comedians go on vacation?
Jokelahoma.

Brittany Martini—Georgia

What is the smartest state?
Alabama, because it has four A's and one B.

Anka Cannon—Mississippi

David: "I was born in Texas."
Allison: "What part?"
David: "All of me, of course."

Ryan Spear—Texas

A tour guide is showing a tourist
 Niagara Falls.
Tour guide: "I'll bet you don't have
 anything like this back in your
 hometown."
Tourist: "No, but we have good
 plumbers who can fix it."

Katie Nelson—Colorado

What is the coldest country in
 South America?
Chile.

Christian Basar—British Columbia

One day a man was lost in the
hills of Kentucky. He stopped and
asked a young boy in a field, "How
do you get to Louisville?"

The boy replied, "My grandpa
takes me!"

Matthew Hall—Indiana

What is the happiest state?
Maryland (Merry land).

Philip Dudley—Ohio

Pietro: "Which is farther—New York City or the moon?"

Joanna: "New York City."

Pietro: "Why do you say that?"

Joanna: "I can see the moon, but I can't see New York City."

Sebastian Hann—Alberta

Ken: "I'm glad I wasn't born in France."

Debbie: "Why?"

Ken: "I don't speak French."

Kevin Farina—Pennsylvania

Teacher: "Who can tell me what the capital of Missouri is?"

Student: "That's easy. It's *M*."

Lauren Beebe—Washington

Teacher: "Jane, can you tell me where the English Channel is?"
Jane: "I'm sorry. We don't get that TV station."

James Brady—Pennsylvania

If Mississippi gave Missouri her New Jersey, what would Delaware?
I don't know, but Alaska.

Ashley Singleton—Alabama

Teacher: "Sue, please spell *Mississippi*."
Sue: "Which one? The state or the river?"

Caitlin McKinzie—Arizona

How did the boy unlock
    the door to the beach?
With the Florida Keys.

Michael Cohen—Virginia

A geography teacher asked Adam to find the Atlantic Ocean on the world map. A few minutes passed, but no answer. Adam was still touching the map everywhere. The teacher asked, "Why are you touching the map?"

"I'm looking for a wet spot where there should be an ocean!" answered Adam.

Nemanja Mulasmajic—Illinois

Who are the three American sisters?
Mary Land, Louisie Anna, and Minnie Sota.

Ryan Matuszeski—New Mexico

Cackle Soup

What makes chicken jokes?
A comedie-hen.

Renee Spence—Maryland

What did the chicken say about the food?
"*Eggsellent!*"

Steven Silber—Delaware

Which side of a chicken has the
   most feathers?
The outside.

Jane: "Why did the chicken cross
   the road?"
Mike: "I don't know. Why?"
Jane: "To get the *Boston Globe*."
Mike: "I don't get it."
Jane: "Neither do I. I get the *New
   York Times*."

Stacia Richards—Massachusetts

Why did Washington cross the
   Delaware?
Because the chicken needed a ride.

Emily Marsh—New York

A chicken went into a library and said to the librarian, "*Baaaaaaaaak, baak, baak.*"

The librarian said, "You want one long book and two short ones?" The chicken nodded.

The chicken walked down the road to the swamp and showed the books to a frog. The frog said, "Read it. Read it. Read it."

Laura Reed—Idaho

Why are chickens stronger than people?
Because people can get chicken pox, but chickens don't get people pox.

Robert Bowie—Pennsylvania

How does a chicken tell time?
One o'cluck, two o'cluck. . . .

Amy Dunton—Washington

Why did the chicken cross the
  playground?
To get to the other slide.

Riley White—Michigan

Why did the chicken cross the book?
To get to the author side.

Heather Phillips—Minnesota

Why can't you bring a chicken to
school?
Because it might use fowl language.

Ryan Lynch—New Jersey

Which vegetable do chickens like
best?
Eggplant.

Todd Kawaguchi—California

Why do chickens lay eggs?
*Because if they dropped them, they
would break.*

Joel Blevins—Kentucky

A chicken crosses the road and enters a diner. He sits next to a man and asks him, "What is your name?"

The man says, "Bond, James Bond. What is your name?"

The chicken says, "Ken, Chick Ken."

Mark Alejandro—New York

Kate: "Our hen can lay an egg four inches long. Can you beat that?"
Jim: "Yes, with an eggbeater."

Eve Maryn—Maryland

Scared Silly

Imagine you are trapped in a
  haunted house. What should
  you do?
Stop imagining.

Amanda Short—Oklahoma

Girl monster: "Mom, the teacher said I was nice, smart, and well-behaved."

Mother monster: "Don't feel bad, dear. You'll do better next semester."

Justin Park—California

Why did the boy carry a clock and a bird on Halloween?

He was going tick-or-tweeting.

Connor McKean—New York

Why do leaves change colors before Halloween?

Because they want to get their costumes ready.

Danissa Lopez—Massachusetts

Where do witches go to get their
   hair done?
The ugly parlor.

Mary Claveria—Nevada

How do monsters tell their futures?
They read their horror-scopes.

Dakota Blair—Delaware

Kelly: "Is our school haunted?"
Ken: "What makes you say that?"
Kelly: "I keep hearing about school spirit."

Evelyn Gonciarz—Massachusetts

Daughter: "It's so hot today. Could you please tell me a ghost story?"
Dad: "Sure, but why?"
Daughter: "Because ghost stories are so chilling."

Jessica Fischman—California

What is a vampire's favorite animal?
A giraffe.

Corey Martin—Iowa

Why did the cyclops stop teaching?
He had only one pupil.

Amy Brandon and Jennifer Miller—Arizona

What is a skeleton's favorite
instrument?
A trombone.

Sam Browne—Massachusetts

What is a vampire's favorite
holiday?
Fangsgiving.

Lauren Woody—Maryland

What is a monster's favorite
cheese?
Monsterella.

Leila Abuzalaf—Hawaii

Why do witches fly on brooms?
*Because they can't find extension
   cords long enough for their
   vacuum cleaners.*

Kristen Fisher—Jamaica

Boy: "Mr. Monster, I would like to have your daughter's hand in marriage."

Mr. Monster: "Either take all of her or none of her."

Ian Haddock—Texas

What would you get if you crossed
   a werewolf with a snowball?
Frostbite.

Mallory Wainwright—Alabama

Why didn't the skeleton cross the
   road?
Because he didn't have any guts.

Danny Reyes—Florida

What is a ghost's favorite ride?
A roller ghoster.

Justin Wong—Hawaii

What did the wind say to the
   ghost?
"Just passing through."

John Mahoney—New Jersey

How many witches does it take to
  change a light bulb?
*Just one, but she changes it into a
  toad.*

Lauren Wallace—Kentucky

Why can't ghosts play baseball in
  the afternoon?
*Because the bats don't come out
  until night.*

Joan Knihnicki and
Meagan Hiton—Massachusetts

What did the coach say to the
  skeletons before the big game?
*"Let's get out there and show them
  what we're made of!"*

Mark Ropel—Wisconsin

What do ghosts eat for breakfast?
Scream of wheat.

Daniel Tew—Georgia

What happened when the monster
    ate the electric company?
He was in shock for a week.

Jeffrey Thibert—Ontario

Why did the tiny ghost join the
  football squad?
*He heard they needed a little team
  spirit.*

Katie Miller—Washington

What does a ghost have in his
  morning coffee?
Scream and sugar.

Marianne Buchanan—Texas

Julia: "Mom! There's a monster
  under my bed!"
Mom: "Tell him to get back in the
  closet where he belongs."

Chris Chung—California

What contest did the witch's broom win?

The sweepstakes.

Rumi Zaidi—Ontario

Boy monster: "I like your pretty blue eyes."

Girl monster: "Why don't you like my green eyes?"

Ashley Nasca—Virginia

Why did the girl ghost haunt baseball fields?

Because diamonds are a ghoul's best friend.

Martha Fincher—Tennessee

What do Hawaiian pumpkins say?
"Happy Hula-ween!"

Justin Brahms—California

What do you call a giant mummy?
Gauzilla.

Chelsea Stump—Florida

What is a monster's favorite game?
Swallow the leader.

Holly Coey—Alabama

Where do ghosts like to haunt?
*Moantana, Wy-oohhh-ming, and
New Hauntshire.*

Will Scheider—Pennsylvania

Why didn't the monster finish the
ten-page book?
He wasn't that hungry.

Sammy Mellema—New York

What do you get when you cross a
Scottish monster with a clock?
The Clock Ness Monster.

Erin Utley—Texas

Which kind of ghost haunts a
  chicken coop?
A poultrygeist.

Will Hailey—Louisiana

Why was the mummy late for
  dinner?
He was wrapped up in his work.

Melissa Wilbur—Massachusetts

Why do witches fly on brooms?
It beats walking.

Amber Snowden—Ohio

What do baby ghosts wear on
  their feet?
Booties.

Brynn Shader—Florida

What does a witch ask for when
  she checks into a hotel?
Broom service.

Joseph Lee—California

Why do we carve pumpkins on
   Halloween?
Ever try carving a grape?

Zack Hann—Georgia

Raccoon: "How are you?"

Rabbit: "Fine, but are you OK?"

Raccoon: "Yes. Why do you ask?"

Rabbit: "Because Halloween was three months ago, and you're still wearing your mask."

Liana Smith—Indiana

Why was the ghost so lonely?
Because it didn't have any body.

Cristina Wadhwa—Ontario

Baby monster: "Look, Mom! I got a jogger for dinner!"

Mother monster: "How many times do I have to say 'No more fast food!'"

Keshia-Lee Martin—New York

Why don't mummies go on
vacation?
*Because they might relax and
unwind.*

Michelle Barnes—Alberta

Old ghost: "I'm going to give up
haunting."
Young ghost: "Why?"
Old ghost: "I don't seem to
frighten people anymore. I
might as well be alive for all
they care."

Elvina Choi—California

Who is the smartest monster?
Frank-Einstein.

Timothy McClelland—Massachusetts

Why did the doctor tell the ghost to
    ride in an elevator going up?
To boost his spirit.

Ray Andre—Michigan

What did the two vampires do from
midnight to 12:10?
They took a coffin break.

Cody Lang—Alberta

First monster: "We must be
getting close to a city."
Second monster: "Why do you
say that?"
First monster: "We're stepping
on more people."

Gina Syarif—California

What did one ghost say to the
other?
"Do you believe in people?"

Jillian Martines—Pennsylvania

Funny Bones

A man once walked into a doctor's office with a pelican on his head.

"You need help immediately," said the doctor.

"I certainly do," replied the pelican. "Get this man out from under me!"

Coye Farmer—Texas

Jeff: "What would you do if you broke your arm in two places?"

Jenny: "I'd stay away from those places."

Haley Smith—Colorado

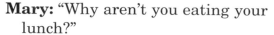

Mary: "Why aren't you eating your lunch?"

Greg: "I'm supposed to take these pills first. My doctor said to take two on an empty stomach."

Mary: "Do they do any good?"

Greg: "I don't know. They keep rolling off my stomach every time I stand up."

Kelly O'Brien—Pennsylvania

Why did Mr. and Mrs. Tonsil dress up?

Because the doctor was taking them out.

Kammi Kroeplin—Oregon

Doctor: "How are you getting along with those strength pills I gave you last week?"

Patient: "I don't know. I'm not strong enough to get the lid off the bottle yet."

Gigi Chan—British Columbia

Nurse: "May I take your pulse?"

Patient: "Why? Haven't you got one of your own?"

Pamela Ting—New Jersey

Toni: "Have you ever seen an oil well?"

Pat: "No, but I've never seen one sick, either."

Shannon Watson—Alberta

What do you call someone who
treats sick ducks?
A ducktor.

Austin Copeland—Colorado

What illness can you catch from a
  martial arts expert?
Kung flu.

Mike Cardosa—Michigan

Nurse: "Your cough sounds better today."

Danny: "It should—I practiced all night."

Larry Li—British Columbia

Mary: "Why are you jumping up and down like that?"

Greg: "I took my medicine but I forgot to shake the bottle."

Daniel Sherman—Maryland

School nurse: "Your poison ivy will be all gone by tomorrow."

Kim: "Please don't make rash promises!"

Caitlin Koehn—Kansas

Mary: "I had an ear infection a
  long time ago."
Beth: "How long ago?"
Mary: "Oh, it was ears ago."

Emily Windram—New Jersey

What does a doctor do with a sick
  zeppelin?
He tries to helium.

Andrew Gendro—Washington

Josh: "Did you know that I had
  a weak back?"
Matt: "When?"
Josh: "About a week back."

Joshua Rodriguez—Virginia

Why was a man wearing a hot pad
  on his head?
He had a head cold.

Michael Urbach—California

If an apple a day keeps the doctor away, what does an onion a day do?

It keeps everyone away.

Amanda Lehigh—Washington

Doctor: "I'm getting angry!"
Nurse: "Well, don't lose your patients."

Jonathan Goodrum—New York

Why did the chimney call the doctor?

Because the fireplace had the flue.

Halea Boswell—Virginia

Science teacher: "Class, did you
know that grasshoppers have
antennae?"

Marianne: "Cool. Do they get
cable?"

Alexis Akey—New York

Teacher: "What happens when the human body is totally submerged in water?"

Debbie: "The telephone rings."

Robert Boord—California

Teacher: "Why aren't you going home for lunch?"
Student: "My father told me not to leave school until I graduate."

Henry Odoi—Ghana

What do you call it when you wake up in the middle of a dream about school?
A half-day.

Christina Scarbel—North Carolina

Teacher: "We will have a half-day of school this morning."
Students: "Hurray! Yippee!"
Teacher: "We will have the other half this afternoon."

Nathan Foppe—Illinois

Why did the student eat his
  homework?
*Because his teacher told him it
  was a piece of cake.*

Shane Smith—Washington

With tears in his eyes, a little boy
told his teacher that only two boots
were left in the classroom and they
weren't his. The teacher searched
and searched, but she couldn't find
any other boots. "Are you sure these
boots aren't yours?" she asked.

"I'm sure," the boy sobbed. "Mine
had snow on them."

Cassandra Mae Hagemann—Idaho

Why couldn't the flower go to
   school on its bike?
Its petals were broken.

Lawrence Dowler—Virginia

What subject do you study at the
  mall?
Buyology.

Hilary Woodcum—Florida

Ann: "Hurray! Our teacher said we would have a test today, rain or shine."

Daniel: "Then why are you so happy?"

Ann: "It's snowing!"

Jeff Kao—California

What is a librarian's favorite food? *Shush-kabob.*

Kendra Feeley—Massachusetts

Teacher: "Tom, what is your favorite food?"

Tom: "Succotash."

Teacher: "OK, spell it."

Tom: "Actually, I like eggs better."

Bud Rimes—New York

Nika: "School is so confusing!"

Dad: "Why?"

Nika: "Ms. Peterson said, 'One plus nine equals ten, six plus four equals ten, and seven plus three equals ten.' "

Dad: "So?"

Nika: "She won't make up her mind!"

Nika Rosen—California

Student: "I don't know what job I should try for. Barbers make more money than some writers, but I love to write stories."

Professor: "Why not flip a coin—heads or tales."

Rhebeka Zoitas—Florida

What is an elf's favorite song to
    sing at school?
The elfabet song.

Kristen Battista—New York

Jim: "Why were you late for school?"

Tom: "There are eight people in our family, and the alarm clock was set for seven."

Margaret Ostrovich—Pennsylvania

Baby-sitter: "What did you learn at school today?"

Yolanda: "I learned to say 'Yes, ma'am,' 'No, ma'am,' 'Yes, sir,' and 'No, sir.'"

Baby-sitter: "You did?"

Yolanda: "Yep."

Amanda Bryden—Delaware

Mellody: "Let's play school."

Suzie: "OK. Let's pretend I'm absent."

Kojo and Jessica Meyer—Virginia

Teacher: "Name two pronouns."

Karen: "Who, me?"

Teacher: "That's correct."

Humphrey Cheung—Ontario

Mom: "How was your first day at school?"

Maria: "OK, but I didn't get my present yet."

Mom: "What present?"

Maria: "Well, the teacher said to me, 'Maria, sit there for the present.' Maybe I'll get it tomorrow."

Jessica Kim—California

Joy: "I packed my own lunch today."

Kelley: "What did you bring?"

Joy: "Uh . . . chocolate soup."

Kelley: "Chocolate soup?"

Joy: "Well, this morning it was ice cream!"

Lisa Samuel—Texas

Student: "Have you heard the joke about the pencil that was broken?"
Teacher: "No."
Student: "It was pointless."

Kathryn Fox
—North Carolina

What animal flies around schools
   at night?
An alpha-bat.

Christin Antonelli—Florida

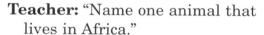

Teacher: "Name one animal that lives in Africa."

Student: "An elephant."

Teacher: "Good! Now try to name another."

Student: "Another elephant."

Payal Shah—Arizona

Teacher: "Could you tell me something about the Iron Age?"

Ernie: "Sorry, I'm a little rusty on that one."

Jiwon Park—Illinois

In what school do you learn how to greet people?

Hi school.

Bonnie Devanath—Virginia

At which school do you have to
    drop out to graduate?
Parachute school.

Eileen Hammond—Georgia

Why shouldn't you ever dot another
    student's *i*'s?
*Because you should keep your eyes
on your own paper.*

Trey Chapman—Oklahoma

Said a boy to his teacher one day,
"Wright has not written *write* right,
I say."

And the teacher replied as the
blunder she eyed, "Right! Wright,
write *write* right, right away!"

Emily Smith—California

Why did the kids go to the White House and look at the trees?
They were studying the branches of government.

Andrea Hempel—Ohio

Why is doing multiplication
  sometimes hard work?
*Because of all those numbers you
  have to carry.*

Teacher: "Why were you late for
  school today, Albert?"
Albert: "I was obeying the sign
  that said Go Slow—School
  Ahead."

Tom Cronin—California

What is a teacher's favorite food?
Graded cheese.

Hailey Hoyt—Oklahoma

Witty Weather

What is worse than raining cats
   and dogs?
Hailing buses.

Michele Kopin—New Jersey

What do clouds wear in their hair?
Rainbows.

Sean Gilmartin—Illinois

What do rain clouds wear under
   their silver linings?
Thunderwear.

James Krips—Pennsylvania

How do you buy a thundercloud?
With a rain check.

Raffaele Esposito—Ontario

First cloud: "When did you take
   your last shower?"
Second cloud: "I don't take
   showers—I give them!"

Audra Leichleiter—Nebraska

What do snowmen ride?
Ice-cycles.

Jill Spratt—Kansas

It was so cold at the North Pole
   that
—our candle froze and we couldn't
   blow it out;
—our words froze and we had to
   wait until summer to hear what
   we'd said.

Cecilia Raassina—France

What should you do when it's
   raining cats and dogs?
Be careful not to step on a poodle.

Alicia Hansel—California

Dan: "I hope the rain keeps up."
Karen: "Why?"
Dan: "So it won't come down."

Madison Dennis—Massachusetts

What do you call a snowman
in June?
A puddle.

Eric Meister—Pennsylvania

What colors go with the sun and
the wind?
The sun rose and the wind blue.

Zach Elbert—Nebraska

Max: "What's the weather like?"
Pam: "I don't know. It's too cloudy
to tell."

Jacob Roatcap—Indiana

What's white and goes up?
A confused snowflake.

Bernice Tracy—Tennessee

What story do snowmen like to tell
their children?
"Coldilocks and the Three Brrrs."

Faye Goodwin—South Carolina

What did the gingerbread boy find
    on his bed?
A cookie sheet.

Mary Helbling—Missouri

A lion was playing checkers with a cheetah. The cheetah skipped across the board and got all the checkers in one move. "You're a cheater!" said the lion.

"You're lion!" said the cheetah.

Brianna Clampitt—Missouri

Katie: "Did you hear about the new corduroy pillows?"

Jim: "Yes. They're making headlines all over town."

Cathy Costello—Minnesota

Tyrene: "Why do you wear your glasses when you sleep?"

Theresa: "So I can see what I'm dreaming."

Terry Wang—Washington

Ashlea: "Did you like the second act of the play?"

Stacey: "I didn't see it. The program said, 'Second Act—Two years later,' so I left."

Ashlea White—Louisiana

How do you find King Arthur in
  the dark?
With a knight light.

Two women bumped into each
other on the sidewalk. The first
woman told the second woman
she had a banana in her ear.

The second woman said, "What
did you say?"

And the first woman told her,
"I said, 'You have a banana in your
ear.'"

The second woman said, "I'm
sorry, I can't hear you—I have a
banana in my ear."

Amber GeBauer—Iowa

Where do people put their camels
  when they are out shopping?
In camelots.

William Carlin—Florida

What happened when the frog
broke down on the highway?
He got toad away.

Jaydale Codrington—Connecticut

A man was walking, then he suddenly stopped and looked at the sky. Another man saw him, stopped, and did the same thing. More people came by and also looked at the sky. Finally, the second man asked the first man, "What are you looking at?"

The first man said, "I don't know about you, but I have a nosebleed!"

Fabiola Miranda—California

Lani: "Yesterday, I saw a man fall off an eighty-foot ladder."
Mom: "Was he hurt?"
Lani: "No, he fell off the bottom rung."

Durlynn Afong—Hawaii

Paige: "No."
Crystal: "Do you believe in mind reading?"

Paige Oliver—Texas

Ryan: "Money doesn't grow on trees."
Adam: "Then why do banks have branches?"

Michael Rybacha—British Columbia

Kim: "I keep dreaming that I'm standing in front of a door with a sign on it. I push and push, but I can't open it."
Bill: "What does the sign say?"
Kim: "Pull."

Justin Wong—California

Where do books sleep?
Under their covers.

Philip Nii Kotey—Ghana

What is hair's favorite dance?
The Tangle.

Kellie McCormack—New York

Dad: "Did you take a bath today, Son?"

Son: "No, I didn't. Is there one missing?"

Liz Hoell—Wisconsin

What is bought by the yard and worn by the foot?

A carpet.

Gregory Green—Illinois

Andrew: "I'm calling to make an appointment with the dentist."

Secretary: "I'm sorry, he's out right now."

Andrew: "Great. When do you expect him to be out again?"

Mandi Ritter—Pennsylvania

Bill: "I fell over twenty feet last night."

Bob: "Wow! Were you hurt?"

Bill: "No—I was just trying to get to my seat at the movies."

Laura Lee Lightwood-Mater—Pennsylvania

What is the only finger you can put in a box of crayons?

Your pinky.

Ben Callow—Florida

Marty: "Do you have any color televisions?"

Store owner: "Yes, we do."

Marty: "Good. I'll take one in green."

Ilenna Elman—Massachusetts

Kenny: "Benny, why are you still standing at the bus stop? I thought I told you to take the Fourteenth Street bus."

Benny: "You did, but only ten have gone by."

Brenda Lee—California

Two men were walking along and one of them fell into a well. The other man knew that the guy couldn't swim, so he called down to him, "Is the well empty?"

A call came from below. "No. I'm in it!"

Michael Green
—Delaware

One eye said to the other eye:
"Just between the two of us, there's
something that smells."

Alex Simko—South Carolina

Bob: "You know that alarm clock
   you gave me?"
Sue: "Yes."
Bob: "I had to take it back. It kept
   waking me up when I was
   sleeping."

Kristin Harding—Maryland

What climbs, then falls, but never
   gets hurt?
Your temperature.

Jennifer Rohrer—Wisconsin

John: "Can you take me to the park on Friday?"

Dad: "Sure, but if it rains on Friday, what will we do?"

John: "Go the day before."

Ray Heldt—Michigan

What's filled with ink and has no hair?
A bald-point pen.

Tiffani Dishner—North Carolina

What do Alexander the Great and Smokey the Bear have in common?
They both have the same middle name.

Kenneth Chu—Florida

Why was the bride crying at her
 wedding?
She didn't marry the best man.

Catherine Lunn—Nova Scotia

Sam: "How much for a haircut?"
Barber: "Five dollars."
Sam: "How much for a shave?"
Barber: "Two dollars."
Sam: "Please shave my hair."

Kavya Kumar—India

What did the detective say when he finished packing his suitcase?
"Case closed!"

Benjamin Heimfeld—Washington

Jack: "I notice that Betty got a job sweeping chimneys."
Nancy: "Yes. The job soots her well."

Karen Speltz—Minnesota

How do billboards talk?
Sign language.

Sheila Kottong—California

What's not right and not wrong?
Left.

Michael Incontrera—New York

Alix: "I bet you think I'm too small to jump higher than this tree."
Beth: "Well, aren't you?"
Alix: "Nope! This tree can't jump at all."

Gabrielle Madson—Washington

What did the big gorilla say when he dialed incorrectly?
"Oops! King Kong rang wrong."

Drew Cochran—Mississippi

Why isn't the phone company going to make telephone poles any longer?
Because they are long enough.

Charlotte Webb—Kentucky

What is the greatest honor a
   dragon can get?
Being voted into the Hall of Flame.

Deanna Dobbs—West Virginia

Apatosaurus: "Do you really like living in that small cave?"

Tyrannosaurus rex: "Sure. I have no room to complain."

Bethany Brewer—Colorado

When is a car not a car?
When it turns into a driveway.

Deann Rubenstein—Pennsylvania

What is a tree's favorite type
   of cheese?
Limb-burger.

Benjamin Jordan—Iowa

Ron: "What is five *Q* plus five *Q*?"
Wilma: "Ten *Q*."
Ron: "You're welcome!"

Omari Weekes—New York

Ted: "Why are frogs happy?"
Rob: "They eat whatever bugs
   them."

Renée Zatzman—Nova Scotia

What kind of gum do scientists chew?

Ex-spearmint gum.

Tony Gies—Texas

A group of hikers was hopelessly lost. They demanded an explanation from their confused guide.

"I thought you said you were the best guide in Maine!" said one of the hikers.

"I am," replied the guide. "But I think we're in Canada now."

Cristen Caballero—Florida

What do you call a chocolate rabbit
   that was in the sun too long?
A runny bunny.

Kristy Uveges—Ohio

If you eat two-thirds of a pie, what
do you have?
An angry mom.

Rebecca Bernstein—New Jersey

Where do you go to take a class in
  making ice cream?
Sundae school.

Christopher Morris—Illinois

Why did the jelly roll?
Because it saw the apple turnover.

Eric Weiss—California

What do you call a house full of
  candy?
Dessert-ed.

Russell Tobias—New York

Man: "May I have a banana
  sundae?"
Waiter: "It's only Tuesday."

Jerry George—South Carolina

What is black and white and red
all over?
*A chocolate sundae with ketchup
on it.*

Mary: "Look, ice-cream sticks!"
Aaron: "They aren't ice-cream
sticks—they're called tongue
depressors."
Mary: "I know. When the ice cream
is gone, your tongue is depressed."

Mary Ewing—Wisconsin

Why did the ice-cream cone read
the newspaper?
To get the latest scoop.

Carly Estock—Pennsylvania

Why were there hammers at the
dinner table?
They were serving pound cake.

Caley Meals—Illinois

Share the Fun

Want us to consider your favorite joke or riddle for publication in *Highlights for Children* magazine?

Send us the funniest joke or the best riddle you've ever heard, with your name, age, and full address (number and street, city or town, state or province, and Zip Code), to:

Laugh Out Loud
Highlights for Children
803 Church Street
Honesdale, Pennsylvania 18431